Another Sommer-Time Story

If Only I Were...

By Carl Sommer
Illustrated by Kennon James

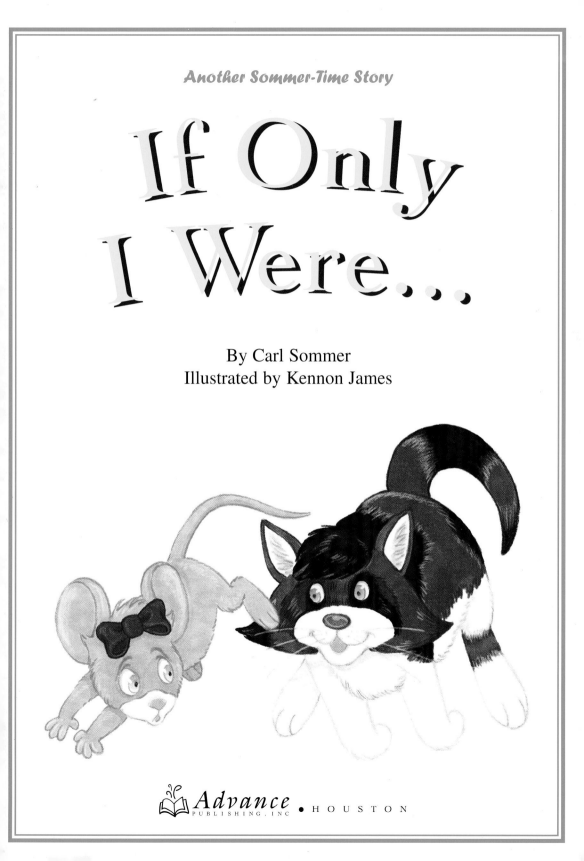

Advance PUBLISHING, INC • HOUSTON

Permissions
Advance Publishing, Inc.
6950 Fulton St.
Houston, TX 77022

http://www.advancepublishing.com

First Edition
Printed in Singapore

Library of Congress Cataloging-in-Publication Data

Sommer, Carl, 1930-
    If only I were— / by Carl Sommer ; illustrated by Kennon James.
  – 1st ed.
      p. cm. – (Another Sommer-time story)
    Summary: As she tries being one creature after another, from a cat to an elephant trainer, Missy the mouse discovers that everyone has problems and that she can find happiness as herself.
    ISBN 1-57537-002-6 (hc : alk. paper). – ISBN 1-57537-051-4 (lib. bdg. : alk. paper)
    [1. Mice–Fiction. 2. Animals–Fiction. 3. Self-acceptance–Fiction.] I. James, Kennon, ill. II. Title. III. Series: Sommer, Carl, 1930- Another Sommer-time story.
PZ7.S696235Ij 1997
[E]–dc20
                                               96-24348
                                                CIP
                                                  AC

If Only I Were...

Once there was a mouse—a wee, little mouse—named Missy.

She had lots of fun, but the wee, little mouse had a very BIG problem.

Food was not the problem. Missy lived with her papa and mama in the zoo-keeper's house— next to the kitchen.

Missy always had something good to eat.

A place to sleep was not the problem.
Missy had a soft little bed in a cozy little room.
At night Papa and Mama would tuck her in and read her a story.

Friends were not the problem.
Around the zoo there were lots of friends...
like lions and tigers and monkeys and bears.

When the visitors went home, the animals had the whole park to themselves. That is when Missy played with her best friends, Itty and Bitty.

Missy *could* have been the happiest mouse in the world...if it had not been for her one BIG problem: Missy did not like being a mouse.

"I'm tired of being so little!" she groaned. "Besides, my ears are too big, and my tail is too skinny!"

Missy dreamed of being like Horace the cat.

Horace also lived in the zoo-keeper's house. To wee little Missy, big Horace seemed like a giant—especially when he chased her.

Missy did not like being chased. "If only I were a big cat," she would say, "I wouldn't have any problems. Then I'd be happy, just like Horace."

Papa and Mama told Missy, "Everyone has problems—even big cats."

But Missy did not think so.

"What problems could Horace have?" she wondered. "He's not little...and he's not ugly. He's big...and strong...and beautiful!"

One night Missy was so sad that she went straight to bed without eating supper.

"It's just not fair!" she cried. "Why do I have to be so little? And why must I have such a skinny tail and big ugly ears?"

Missy finally drifted off to sleep, moaning and groaning, "If only I were like Horace!"

"Here we go again!" huffed Missy. Horace was chasing her. Today was starting out just like every other day. Poor Missy was so tired of being a tiny little mouse.

While running away, Missy wished out loud, "If only I were...a great, big cat!"

Suddenly, to her surprise, her wish came true! Missy turned into a big cat!

Horace put out his feet and came to a sudden stop. "Wh—wh—what happened to Missy? Wh—wh—where did this big cat come from?"

Missy arched her back and gave a loud, "Hsssss...!"

Horace ran away as fast as he could.

Missy licked her paw and swished her new fluffy tail. "It happened! It really happened!"

She smiled and purred, "I'm the biggest and most beautiful cat in the whole world!"

Missy knew just what to do. Like all the other cats, she began chasing Itty and Bitty.

"This is fun!" she laughed while running after her friends.

Missy felt like a giant.

Missy raised her beautiful tail and strutted through the park.

"No more problems for me!" she thought.

But as she rounded the zoo-keeper's house, there in the shade sat a great big dog.

"Ruff! Ruff!" barked the dog. Missy got so scared, she jumped into the air.

Then the big barking dog began chasing her. Missy ran as fast as she could, darting here and there. "Being a cat isn't much fun!" she thought.

Suddenly she got an idea. "I'll try another wish. If only I were...a tiger!"

Suddenly Missy became a tiger.

When the dog saw he was chasing a tiger, he stopped in his tracks.

Missy knew just what to do. She turned around and began chasing the not-so-big dog. "This is fun!" she roared.

Missy pranced around holding her head high. "Now my problems are gone for sure! I don't have to be afraid of anything!"

As she roamed through the park, she made friends with some tigers.

"I have an idea," Missy told her new friends. "Let's have some fun and tease the elephants."

"That's a great idea!" said the tigers. Silently they crept near the herd—then one of the elephants spotted them.

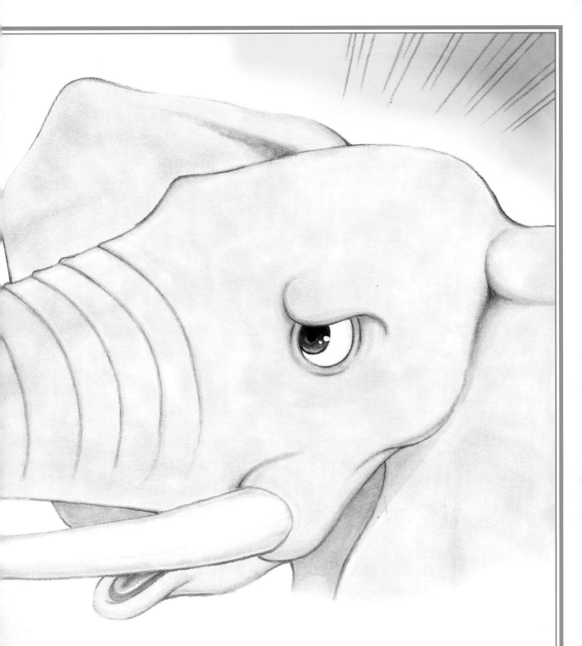

Quickly the elephant spun around and grabbed Missy.

"Please!" begged Missy, "Please! Put me down!"

The elephant ignored Missy's cry and lifted her high in the air.

Then all of a sudden he tossed Missy into a nearby pond. Missy raised her head and shook the water from her ears.

Missy was scared. She jumped out of the water and ran away. "Being a tiger isn't much fun!" she thought. "If only I were...a giant elephant!"

All at once Missy became a giant elephant. Now she felt like the biggest creature in the whole world. "No more problems for me!" she thought. "Surely no one can bother me now!"

Missy the elephant was so big the ground shook as she walked. "I'm the biggest and most powerful creature in the whole world!" she bellowed. "This is fun! *Now* I can go anywhere and no one can stop me!"

Missy did not know it, but some men had come to the zoo to buy an elephant. They needed a big elephant to train for the circus.

The men looked at all the elephants. Then one of them pointed at the biggest and said, "She'd sure make a fine circus elephant."

"But how can we get her?" asked another.

The zoo-keeper thought for a moment, then he said, "I know how."

The zoo-keeper got a bucket full of peanuts and walked over to Missy. Peanuts were Missy's favorite food. When Missy saw the peanuts, she hurried after the zoo-keeper...right into the back of a big truck.

"Mmm! Mmm!" mumbled Missy as she began munching on the peanuts. "Am I ever lucky. Now I can eat as many as I want!"

All at once there was a loud noise. Missy looked up just in time to see the door being slammed shut!

Missy was trapped...and alone...and scared.

"Where are they taking me?" she cried as the truck sped away.

Finally the bouncing truck stopped. The men led Missy out and chained her to a pole.

Before Missy knew it, in came an elephant trainer cracking her whip.

"Come on!" shouted the woman. "You're going to learn to do tricks!"

But Missy did not like doing tricks.

"Being a strong elephant isn't much fun at all!" cried Missy. When the woman left, Missy wished real hard, "If only I were...an elephant trainer!"

Suddenly Missy became an elephant trainer!
She knew just what to do. She went into the
circus tent and made the elephants do all sorts
of things. They had to stand on their back legs,
stand on top of a ladder, hold a ball, and do
many other hard tricks.

"This is fun," thought Missy. "Surely now all my problems are gone! I can make the biggest animals obey me!"

Missy felt very, very powerful.

Just then the ring master came in. "These elephants can do much better tricks than that!" he yelled. "Either you teach them some new tricks, or you're fired!"

Missy did not like being yelled at.

Sadly, Missy headed for the trainer's tent to eat supper. "Being an elephant trainer isn't much fun at all!" thought Missy.

Just as she was about to set her food down, a wee, little mouse ran across the floor—right between her feet!

"E-e-e-e-k!" shouted Missy as she dropped her food. "If only I were . . . a mouse!"

Suddenly Missy became a mouse.

And just as she saw herself change into a mouse, Missy woke up.

"I've been dreaming!" she yelled as she clapped her hands.

Missy jumped out of bed and ran to take a peek at Horace.

"Yippee!" she shouted. "I *am* a mouse!"

Missy was so happy! She discovered that
EVERYONE has problems. Mice have problems
with cats, cats have problems with dogs, dogs
have problems with tigers, tigers have problems
with elephants, elephants have problems with
people, and people have problems with mice.

Missy decided not to be sad anymore about being so little. And she did not even mind looking like a mouse—big ears, skinny tail, and all.

Missy became a very happy mouse. She still had to be careful. But now, whenever she saw Horace, she just stayed home.

When Horace left, then she would go out to play.

Best of all, never again was she sad about the way she looked, or about being...a wee, little mouse.